I0703411

My Family
Says Goodbye to Grandma

Written by Larry Burks

Illustrated by Larry Burks - AI-assisted with love

Little Dusty Books

Lubbock, Texas

Published by Little Dusty Books

www.larryburkswritings.com

Printed in the United States of America
First Edition – 2025

ISBN: 978-1-968636-99-9

Cover and illustrations created with AI-assisted tools and lovingly curated by the author.

Grandma always called me her sunshine.

Every Sunday, we made cinnamon toast. She'd pat the butter until it melted just right. Then we'd sit at the table, and she'd tell me stories about when Daddy was little and had too many frogs in his pocket.

Her hugs smelled like peppermint and laundry soap.

But one day, Grandma stayed in bed.
Daddy said she was very tired.

He said sometimes, when people get very old or very sick, their
bodies stop working the way they should.

We didn't make toast that Sunday.

The next time we saw her, she was in the hospital.
She had blankets tucked up to her chin.
I held her hand.
It felt soft and still, like holding a bird that didn't fly anymore

.

I told her she could rest if she wanted.
She smiled a little.
Then she closed her eyes.

She didn't open them again.

Daddy's shoulders shook. Mommy covered her face with her hands. I didn't understand right away, but then my chest started to feel heavy and hot.

I cried too.

"Why is everyone crying?" I asked.

Mommy knelt beside me. Her face was wet.
"Because we're sad," she said. "We love Grandma so much. And now that she's gone, we won't get to see her again. That makes our hearts hurt."

Later, I asked, "Is she gone like my puppy was? Like... I won't see her again?"

Daddy pulled me close. "That's right, just like that. But the love we have, that part doesn't go away."

He pointed to my heart.
"She's right here now. Every time you laugh, every time you tell her stories... she's with you."

At the church, people wore dark clothes and quiet faces.
Someone gave me a flower. I didn't want to let go of it.

People hugged me.

Some told funny Grandma stories. I liked those best.

Now, sometimes I wake up and smell cinnamon toast—even when we haven't made any.

Sometimes the wind sounds like Grandma humming her song.

I still miss her.

But I never think about the sad parts.
I think about frogs in pockets, toast on Sundays, and peppermint hugs.
And that makes me happy.

A Note from Pappy

Pappy writes these books because he cares about families,
especially *yours*.
Sometimes life is hard to understand, but you are never alone.
You are loved.
You are strong.
And Pappy believes in you.

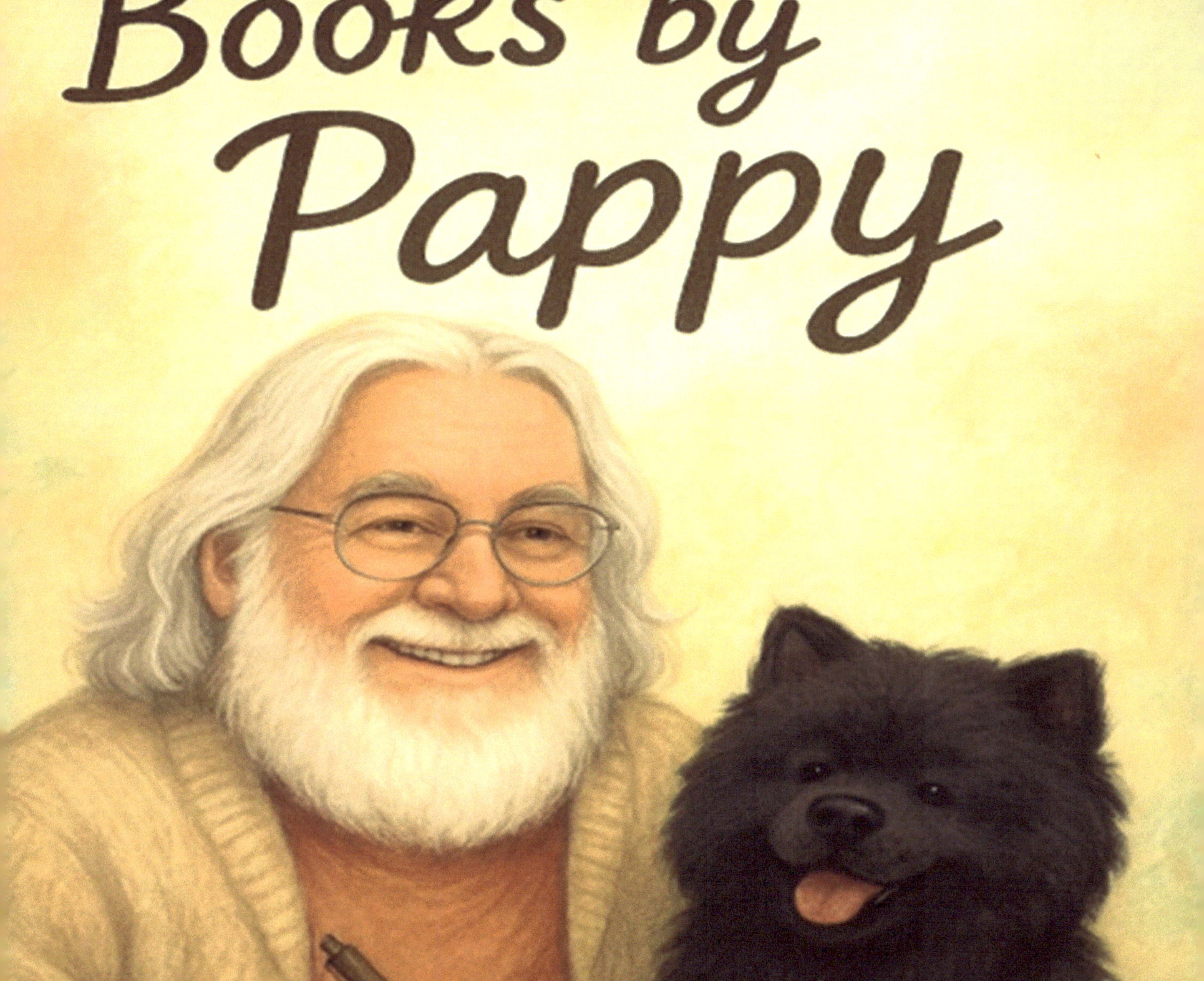
Books by
Pappy

Note to: Parent / Pastor / Teacher / Therapist

This book is just one chapter in a growing five-book collection designed to help kids (and the grown-ups who love them) tackle life's trickiest moments with warmth and honesty. Look for these other titles:

- *My Family Says Adoption Is Love*
- *My Family Is More Than One Color*
- *My Family Lives Apart*
- *My Family Has Someone in a Wheelchair*

You can grab digital companion printables for **My Family Says Goodbye to Grandma**—including coloring pages, memory-jar tags, and an activity sheet, at **www.larryburkswritings.com**. Print them, share them, and keep the conversation going long after story-time ends.

Thank you for guiding children through big feelings and tough questions. This series will keep expanding to meet families where they are. Upcoming sets (titles may shift before publication) are expected to include:

- ✅ *My Family Has a New Baby*
- ✅ *My Family Misses Our Pet*
- ✅ *My Family Taught Me Body Safety*
- ✅ *My Family Has Someone Who's Sick*
- ✅ *My Family Helped Me Feel Safe at School*
- ✅ *My Family Can't Do Fun Stuff*
- ✅ *My Family Said Goodbye to Our House*
- ✅ *My Family Helped My Friend Be Safe*
- ✅ *My Family Has Two Dads / Two Mommies*

Each forthcoming book will pair gentle storytelling with practical resources—because every child deserves clear answers, steady support, and a safe place to grow.